VEGGIES
with
WEDGIES

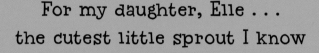

For my daughter, Elle . . .
the cutest little sprout I know

LITTLE SIMON

An imprint of Simon & Schuster Children's Publishing Division
1230 Avenue of the Americas, New York, New York 10020
Copyright © 2014 by Todd H. Goldman
All rights reserved, including the right of reproduction in whole
or in part in any form. LITTLE SIMON is a registered trademark of
Simon & Schuster, Inc., and associated colophon is a trademark of
Simon & Schuster, Inc. For information about special discounts for
bulk purchases, please contact Simon & Schuster Special Sales at
1-866-506-1949 or business@simonandschuster.com.
The Simon & Schuster Speakers Bureau can bring authors to your
live event. For more information or to book an event contact the
Simon & Schuster Speakers Bureau at 1-866-248-3049 or visit our
website at www.simonspeakers.com. Designed by Laura Roode
Manufactured in China 0318 SCP

4 6 8 10 9 7 5

Library of Congress Cataloging-in-Publication Data
Doodler, Todd H. Veggies with wedgies / by Todd H. Doodler. –
First edition. pages cm Summary: The vegetables in Farmer John's
garden are intrigued when he hangs his underwear out to dry but
when Corn, Potato, Beet, and the others pull things off the line and
try them on, they are not at all comfortable.
ISBN 978-1-4424-9340-7 (hardcover : alk. paper) –
ISBN 978-1-4424-9341-4 (ebook) [1. Underwear–Fiction.
2. Vegetables–Fiction. 3. Clothing and dress–Fiction. 4. Farm life–
Fiction. 5. Humorous stories.] I. Title. PZ7.D7247Veg 2014
[E]–dc23 2013006905

VEGGIES with WEDGIES

Written and Illustrated by

Todd H. Doodler

LITTLE SIMON

New York London Toronto Sydney New Delhi

Every morning Farmer John hung his family's clothes to dry in the warm sunlight, right above the vegetable garden. Usually there were shirts and pants and some fluffy bath towels.

One day Farmer John was drying something different,
and that got the attention of some very curious vegetables.

"They look silly to me," said Mushroom.
"Maybe we should get some!" said Asparagus.
"But we don't even know what they are!" cried Onion.

"What is everyone talking about?" asked Corn.

"Look!" said Tomato. "Up there!"

"We're trying to find out what those are!" said Potato.

"Maybe they are socks!" said Pea. "For your feet!"

"But socks don't have holes in them," said Broccoli.

"My socks do!" said Asparagus.

"Maybe they are hats!" said Mushroom.

"They don't look like hats," said Tomato.

"Why is everyone staring at Farmer John's underwear?" asked Carrot.

"Underwear?" said Beet.
"What's underwear?"
"Does it come from the
underwear fairy?" asked Pea.

"No!" said Pumpkin.
"You trick-or-treat for
underwear!"

"No, no, no!" said Carrot. "Underwear is clothing that people wear under their clothes. **Under wear**, Get it?"
The veggies thought about this for a while.

"Can we wear underwear?" asked Pea.
"But we don't wear clothes!" said Tomato. "We have nothing to wear our underwear under!!"
The veggies were sad for a moment.
"I don't see why we couldn't wear them anyway," said Carrot.
The vegetables perked up.

"But where are we going to get underwear?" asked Potato.
"Well maybe we could borrow Farmer John's," said Carrot.
"Just to try them."

The veggies agreed this was an
excellent idea. So they set about
getting them down.

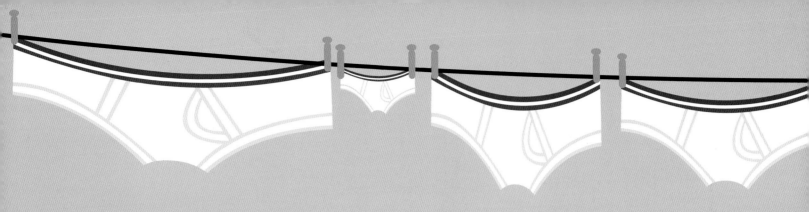

This took a bit of work.

Finally the veggies pulled down the underwear.
They were very excited to try them on.

Mushroom put the underwear
on his head.

"That's not how you wear it!"
said Carrot.

Beet put the underwear
on his arm.

"That's not right either!"
said Carrot.

Corn put the underwear
over his ears.

"That's not right at all!"
said Carrot.

**"You put on
underwear like THIS!"**

He put on the underwear
and proudly turned around.

Then the veggies each hopped
and wiggled their way into a pair.

It took a little bit of hopping

and a **lot** of wiggling.

Soon the veggies were all wearing underwear.
Then they were all very quiet.

Potato spoke first. "This is not comfortable!" he cried.

"Not at all!" said Beet.

"I want it off!" wailed Tomato.

"Something is not right!" said Carrot.

The veggies all had terrible

wedgies!

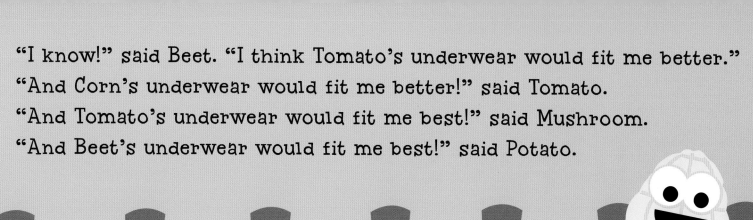

"I know!" said Beet. "I think Tomato's underwear would fit me better."
"And Corn's underwear would fit me better!" said Tomato.
"And Tomato's underwear would fit me best!" said Mushroom.
"And Beet's underwear would fit me best!" said Potato.

So all the veggies traded underwear.
Then they hopped and wiggled their way into different pairs.

"Much better!" said Potato.

"Perfect!" said Beet, twirling around.

"Mine feel just right!" said Corn.

"All better!" said Broccoli.

"Oh, I could just do a dance," said Pea.

And the veggies sang and danced to their new underwear song:

"Oh, underwear is so fine,
I want to wear it all the time.
Underwear, it is the best.
Just find the pair that fits you
better than the rest."

From that day on, the veggies hopped and wiggled and put on their underwear whenever Farmer John wasn't watching. The veggies were very happy and mostly didn't have any more wedgies.

Except for a few.

And Farmer John is still looking for his underwear.

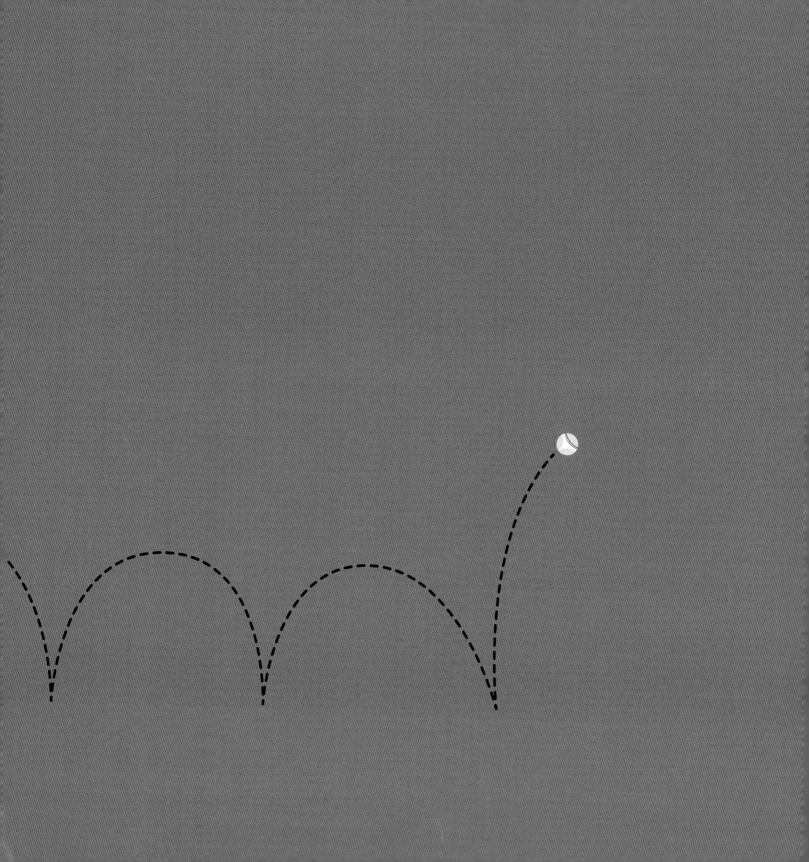